George Be

Candida

Adapted and Abridged by
Aurand Harris

Single copies of plays are sold for reading purposes only. The copying
or duplicating of a play, or any part of play, by hand or by any other
process, is an infringement of the copyright. Such infringement will be
vigorously prosecuted.

Baker's Plays
7611 Sunset Blvd.
Los Angeles, CA 90042
bakersplays.com

NOTICE

CAST

REVEREND JAMES MORELL

MISS PROSERPINE GARNETT (Prossy)

REVEREND ALEXANDER MILL (Lexy)

MRS. JAMES MORELL (Candida)

EUGENE MARCHBANKS

TIME: A day in October, 1894.

SCENE: The drawing room, St. Dominic's Parsonage, London.

Candida

SCENE: *The drawing room of St. Dominic's Parsonage, London, 1894. There is a large window at back, in front of which is a long table, littered with phamphlets, letters, and the like. A chair is at the end of the table. This is where* REVEREND MORELL *does his work. On a smaller table is a typewriter. This is where his typist does her work. On the right wall is a fireplace with a chair and sofa near it. A door leading to the dining area is by the fireplace. A larger doorway is on the opposite side, leading to the front hall and stairs. There are bookshelves, bric-a-brac, but nothing useless or pretentious in the room, money being too scarce in the house of an east end parson to be wasted on snobbish trimmings.*

The REVEREND JAMES MORELL *sits in his chair at the end of the table. He is a vigorous, genial, popular man of forty, robust and goodlooking, full of energy, with pleasant, hearty, considerate manners, and a sound unaffected voice, which he uses with the clear athletic articulation of a practised orator, and with a wide range and perfect command of expression.*

The typist, MISS PROSERPINE GARNETT, *is a brisk little woman about thirty, neatly but cheaply dressed, notably pert and quick of speech and not very civil in her manner. She is clattering away busily at her machine whilst* MORELL *opens the last of his morning's letters. He reads its content with a comic groan of despair.*

PROSERPINE. Another lecture?

5

MORELL. Yes. The Hoxton Freedom Group wants me to address them on SUNDAY morning. (*Hands her letter*) Tell them to come to church if they want to hear me on Sunday.

PROSERPINE. Oh, they are only half a dozen ignorant costermongers without five shillings between them.

MORELL. (*Amused*) Ah, but you see they're near relatives of mine.

PROSERPINE. Relatives of yours!

MORELL. Yes. We have the same father—in Heaven.

PROSERPINE. (*Relieved*) Oh, is that all?

(*As they continue to work, their proceedings are enlivened by the entrance of the* REVEREND ALEXANDER MILL, *a young graduate of Oxford who is giving the east end of London the benefit of his University training. He is a conceitedly well intentioned, enthusiastic immature novice.* MORELL *looks up indulgently*)

MORELL. Well, Lexy? Late again, as usual.

LEXY. I'm afraid so.

PROSERPINE. You have all the work to do this afternoon.

LEXY. Is she in earnest, Morell?

MORELL. Yes. My wife's coming up for two days.

LEXY. But if the children had scarlatina, do you think it wise—

MORELL. Scarlatina! Rubbish! It was German measles. I brought it into the house myself from the Pycroft Street School. A parson is like a doctor, my boy; he must face infection as a soldier must face bullets. Catch the measles if you can, Lexy: my wife will nurse you; and what a piece of luck that will be for you! Eh?

LEXY. (*Smiles uneasily*) It's so hard to understand you about Mrs. Morell—

MORELL. Ah, my boy, get married to a good woman; and then you'll understand. That's a foretaste of what will be best in the Kingdom of Heaven. And it will cure you of being late. An honest man feels that he must pay Heaven for every hour of happiness with a good spell of hard work to make others happy. Get a wife like my Candida! (*Exits* R, *with some papers*)

LEXY. What a good man! What a thorough loving soul he is!

PROSERPINE. Oh, a man ought to be able to be fond of his wife without making a fool of himself about her. Candida here, and Candida there, and Candida everywhere! It's enough to drive anyone out, of their senses to hear a woman raved about in that absurd manner merely because she's got good hair and a tolerable figure.

LEXY. I had no idea you had any feeling against Mrs. Morell.

PROSERPINE. I have no feeling against her. She's very nice, very good-hearted. I'm very fond of her. Now, about your work. Here's a list for the afternoon. (LEXY *starts to leave at* L)

MORELL. (*Rushes in from* R) Is that a carriage I hear?

LEXY. (*Exiting at* L) It's a cab stopping in front. It's Mrs. Morell.

MORELL. Candida here already! (*Crosses to doorway*)

CANDIDA. (*Enters* L) Yes, James. I'm here. I'm home.

(*She is a woman of thirty-three, with the double charm of youth and motherhood. Her ways are those of a woman who has found that she can always manage people by engaging their affection, and who does so frankly and instinctively without the smallest scruple; but her courage, largeness of mind and dignity of character ennobles her cunningness*)

MORELL. Candida! My—my darling! I intended to meet you at the train. I was so engrossed— I forgot— Oh! (*He embraces her with penitent emotion*) My poor love. How did you manage about the luggage? How—

CANDIDA. There! There! There! I wasn't alone. Eugene has been down with us; and we traveled together.

MORELL. (*Pleased*) Eugene!

CANDIDA. Yes. He's struggling with my luggage, poor boy. Go out, dear, at once, or he'll pay for the cab, and I don't want that. (MORELL *rushes out at* L)

PROSERPINE. Welcome home, Mrs. Morell.

CANDIDA. I didn't see you, Miss Garnett. It's good to be back, even for just a few days.

PROSERPINE. I'll tell Maria you have arrived.

CANDIDA. (*Looking out window*) Poor Eugene. He's so shy.

PROSERPINE. He can't be too poor. His uncle is an earl.

CANDIDA. Oh, he's a dear boy. We are very fond of him. (PROSERPINE *nods and exits* R) Come in, Eugene. (MARCHBANKS *enters at* L. *He is a strange, shy youth of eighteen, with a shrinking manner that shows the painful sensitiveness of very swift and acute apprehensiveness in youth, before the character has grown to its full strength*) Why so sad? And why were you so melancholy in the cab?

MARCHBANKS. I was wondering how much I ought to give the cabman. But it's all right. He beamed all over when Morell gave him two shillings. I was on the point of offering him ten.

(MORELL *enters* L)

CANDIDA. Oh, James, dear, he was going to give the cabman ten shillings! Ten shillings for a three minute drive! Oh, dear!

MORELL. Never mind, Marchbanks. The overpaying instinct is a generous one.

MARCHBANKS. No: cowardice, incompetence. Mrs. Morell's quite right.

CANDIDA. Of course she is. (*Takes up handbag*) And now I must leave you to James for the present. I suppose you are too much of a poet to know the state a woman finds her house in when she's been away for three weeks. Give me my rug. (EUGENE *does*) Now hang my cloak across my arm. (*He does*) Now my hat. Now open the door for me. (*He does*) Thank you.

(*She exits* L)

MORELL. You'll stay to dinner, Marchbanks, of course.

MARCHBANKS. I mustn't. I mean I can't.

MORELL. You mean you won't.

MARCHBANKS. No: I should like to, indeed. Thank you very much. But—but—

MORELL. But—but—Bosh! If you'd like to stay, stay.

MARCHBANKS. The truth is, Mrs. Morell told me not to. She said she didn't think you'd ask me to stay, but that I was to remember, if you did, that you didn't really want me to. She said I'd understand; but I don't. Please don't tell her I told you.

MORELL. (*With affectionate seriousness*) My dear lad, in a happy marriage like ours, there is something very sacred in the return of the wife to her home. (EUGENE *reacts with a horror-stricken expression*) Candida thought I would rather not have you here; but she was wrong. I'm very fond of you, my boy, and I should like you to see for yourself what a happy thing it is to be married as I am.

MARCHBANKS. Happy! Your marriage! You think that! You believe that!

MORELL. (*Buoyantly*) I know it, my lad.

MARCHBANKS. (*Wildly*) No: it isn't true. I'll force it into the light.

MORELL. Force what?

MARCHBANKS. There is something that must be settled between us. You think yourself stronger than I am; but I shall stagger you if you have a heart in your breast.

MORELL. (*Powerfully confident*) Stagger me, my boy. Out with it.

MARCHBANKS. First—

MORELL. First?

MARCHBANKS. I love your wife.

MORELL. (*Amazed, then bursts into laughter*) Why, my dear child, of course you do. Everybody loves her: they can't help it. I like it. But—Eugene, you're under twenty: she's over thirty. Doesn't it look rather like a case of calf love?

MARCHBANKS. You dare say that of her! You think that way of the love she inspires! It is an insult to her.

MORELL. (*Also angry*) To her! Take care. I am being patient. I hope to remain patient. Don't force me to show you the indulgence I should show to a child. Be a man.

MARCHBANKS. Oh, let us put aside all that cant. It horrifies me when I think of the doses, the sermons, she has had to endure all these years with you. You! You, who have not one thought—one sense—in common with her.

MORELL. (*Philosophically*) She seems to bear it pretty well. (*Seriously*) My boy, you are making a fool of yourself. It is easy to shake a man's faith in himself. To take advantage of that, to break a man's spirit is devil's work.

MARCHBANKS. I told you I should stagger you.

MORELL. (*They confront one another threateningly for a moment. Then* MORELL *recovers his dignity*) Eugene, listen to me. Some day I hope and trust you will be a happy man, a happy married man like me. (MORELL *controls himself at* EUGENE's *reaction, and continues with great artistic beauty of delivery*) You can be one of the makers of the Kingdom of Heaven on earth; and —who knows? —you may be a master builder where I am only a humble journey-man. It should make you tremble to think that the heavy burden and great gift of a poet may be laid upon you.

MARCHBANKS. It does not make me tremble. It is the want of it in others that makes me tremble.

MORELL. (*Redoubling his force of style*) Then help to kindle it in them—in me—not to extinguish it. In the future, when you are as happy as I am, I will be your true brother in the faith.

MARCHBANKS. Is it always like this for her? Preach! Preach! Preach! Do you think a woman's soul can live on your talent for preaching?

MORELL. (*Stung*) Marchbanks: you make it hard for me to control myself. My talent is like yours, the gift of finding words for divine truth.

MARCHBANKS. It's the gift of gab, nothing more and nothing less. I've been to your political meetings; when you rouse the men to behave exactly as if they were drunk. And their wives looked on and saw what fools they were. Oh, it's an old story: you'll find it in the Bible. I imagine King David, in his fits of enthusiasm, was very like you. "But his wife despised him in her heart."

MORELL. Leave my house. Do you hear? (*Advances on him threateningly*)

MARCHBANKS. (*Shrinks back*) Let me alone. Don't touch me. (MORELL *grabs him powerfully by the lapel of his coat*) Stop, Morell. Let me go!

MORELL. (*With slow emphatic scorn*) You little sniveling cowardly whelp. (*Releases him*) Go, before you frighten yourself into a fit.

MARCHBANKS. (*Relieved by the withdrawal of* MORELL's *hand*) I'm not afraid of you. It's you who are afraid of me.

MORELL. (*Quietly, as he stands over him*) It looks like it, doesn't it?

MARCHBANKS. You think because I can't lift a heavy trunk down from the top of a cab like you——because I can't fight you for your wife as a drunken navvy would: all that makes you think I'm afraid of you! But you're wrong. I'll fight your ideas. I'll rescue her from her slavery to them. You are driving me out of the house because you daren't let her choose between your ideas and mine. Send me away. Tell her how you were strong and manly, and shook me as a terrier shakes a rat.

MORELL. (*Puzzled*) Why do you want her to know this?

MARCHBANKS. (*With lyric rapture*) Because she will understand me, and know that I understand her. If you keep back one word of truth from her, then you will know to the end of your days that she really belongs to me and not to you. Goodbye, Mr. Clergyman. (*As he turns to door,* CANDIDA *enters at* L)

CANDIDA. Are you going, Eugene? (*Looks observantly at him*) Well, dear me, just look at you. You are a poet, certainly. Look at him, James! Look at his collar! Look at his tie! Look at his hair! One would think somebody had been throttling you. Here! Stand still! (*She tidies him up*) There! Now you look so nice that I think you'd better stay for dinner after all, though I told you you mustn't. (*She puts a final touch to the bow tie. He kisses her hand*) Don't be silly.

MARCHBANKS. I want to stay, of course; unless the reverend gentleman, your husband, has anything to advance to the contrary.

CANDIDA. Shall he stay, James, if he promises to be a good boy and help me to lay the table?

MORELL. (*Shortly*) Oh yes, certainly: he had better stay. (*Starts off* L)

CANDIDA. I'll call you when it's time to help me. (*Holds out her hands to* MARCHBANKS. *He holds them. She exits at* R)

MARCHBANKS. (*Holds his hands which have touched hers to his heart*) I am the happiest of mortals.

MORELL. So was I—an hour ago.

(*He exits* L)

MARCHBANKS. (*Alone, repeats her name*) Candida . . . Candida . . . (*Sees typewriter, pecks out her name with one finger*) C--a--n--d-- (*Hits wrong key and suddenly the carriage shoots across with a bang. Worried, he starts turning knobs and wheels*)

PROSERPINE. (*Enters* R) What are you doing with my typewriter, Mr..Marchbanks?

MARCHBANKS. I'm very sorry,. Miss Garnett. I only tried to make it write.

PROSERPINE. You have altered the spacing.

MARCHBANKS. I only turned a little wheel. It gave a sort of click.

PROSERPINE. (*Fixes typewriter*) I suppose you thought it was a sort of barrel-organ. Nothing to do but turn the handle, and it would write a poem for you straight off, eh?

MARCHBANKS. (*Seriously*) I suppose a machine could be made to write a poem—a love letter.

PROSERPINE. How would I know?

MARCHBANKS. I thought clever people, like you, who can do business and type letters—always had to have love affairs to keep them from going mad.

PROSERPINE. (*Outraged*) Mr. Marchbanks!

MARCHBANKS. Perhaps I shouldn't have alluded to your love affairs.

PROSERPINE. I haven't any love affairs.

MARCHBANKS. Really! Then you are shy, like me.

PROSERPINE. Certainly I am not shy.

MARCHBANKS. (*Secretly*) You must be: that is the reason there are so few love affairs in the world. We all go about longing for love: it is our first need, the first prayer of our hearts; but we dare not utter our longing; we are too shy. (*Very earnestly*) Oh, Miss Garnett, what would you not give to be without fear, without shame—

PROSERPINE. (*Scandalized*) Well, upon my word!

MARCHBANKS. Don't be afraid to be your real self with me. I am just like you. (*Mysteriously*) I go about in search of love. But when I try to ask for it, this horrible shyness strangles me. And I see the affection I am longing for given to dogs and cats and pet birds, because they come and ask for it. (*Whispers*) It must be asked for: it is like a ghost; it cannot speak unless it is first spoken to. (*Usual voice, with deep melancholy*) All the love in the world is longing to speak; only it dare not, because it is shy! shy! shy! That is the world's tragedy.

PROSERPINE. You must stop talking like this, Mr. Marchbanks. It is not proper.

MARCHBANKS. (*Hopelessly*) Nothing that's worth saying is proper.

PROSERPINE. Then hold your tongue.

MARCHBANKS. But does that stop the cry of your heart?

PROSERPINE. It's no business of yours whether my heart cries or not. But I have a mind to tell you, for all that. But if you ever say I said so, I'll deny it.

MARCHBANKS. I know. And so you haven't the courage to tell him?

PROSERPINE. Him? Who?

MARCHBANKS. The man you love. It might be anybody. The young curate, perhaps.

PROSERPINE. Mr. Mill! I'd rather have you than him.

MARCHBANKS. No, really: I'm very sorry; but you mustn't think of that. I—

PROSERPINE. (*Testily*) Oh, don't be frightened: it's not you. It's not any one particular person.

MARCHBANKS. I know. You feel that you could love anybody that offered—

PROSERPINE. (*Exasperated*) Anybody that offered! No, I do not. What do you take me for?

MARCHBANKS. It's no use. You won't make me real answers: only those things that everybody says.

PROSERPINE. Well, if you want original conversation, wait until Mr. Morell comes. He'll talk to you. Oh, you needn't make wry faces over him. He can talk better than you. (*With temper*) Yes! He'd talk your little head off.

MARCHBANKS. (*Suddenly enlightened*) Ah! I understand now. Your secret. Tell me: is it really and truly possible for a woman to love him?

PROSERPINE. Well!!

MARCHBANKS. No: answer me. I must know. I can see nothing in him but words, sermons, preaching! You can't love that.

PROSERPINE. I simply don't know what you're talking about.

MARCHBANKS. You do. You lie.

PROSERPINE. Oh!

MARCHBANKS. Is it possible for a woman to love him?

PROSERPINE. (*Looks him straight in the face*) Yes. (*He turns away with a gasp*) Whatever is the matter with you?

CANDIDA. (*Is heard as she enters, carrying an oil reading lamp*) If you stay with us, Eugene, I think I will hand over the cleaning of the lamps to you. (*Rescued, PROSERPINE makes a quiet exit L*)

MARCHBANKS. You have soiled your hands! Yes, I will stay on one condition: that you hand over all the rough and dirty work to me.

CANDIDA. That is very gallant; but I think I should like to see how you do it first. (*Goes to door at L and calls*)

MARCHBANKS. Your beautiful fingers dabbling in paraffin oil!

CANDIDA. James . . . ? James, where are you?

MORELL. (*Off*) Coming, dear.

CANDIDA. You have not been looking after the house properly.

MORELL. (*Entering*) What have I done—or not done—my love?

CANDIDA. My own particular pet scrubbing brush has been used for blacking your shoes.

MARCHBANKS. (*Gives a wail of horror*) You, scrubbing with a brush.

CANDIDA. What is it, Eugene? Are you ill?

MARCHBANKS. Soiling your hands with a scrubbing brush.

CANDIDA. Never mind. Wouldn't you like to present me with a nice new one, with an ivory back inlaid with mother-of-pearl?

MARCHBANKS. (*Soft and musically*) No, not a scrubbing brush, but a boat to sail away in, far from here, where the marble floors are washed by the rain and dried by the sun; where the lamps are stars and don't need to be filled with paraffin oil every day.

MORELL. (*Harshly*) And where there is nothing to do but to be idle, selfish, and useless.

CANDIDA. (*Jarred*) Oh, James! How could you spoil it all?

MARCHBANKS. (*Firing up*) Yes, to be idle, selfish, and useless: that is, to be beautiful and free and happy. Hasn't every man desired that for the woman he loves? That's my deal: what's yours? Sermons and scrubbing brushes!

CANDIDA. (*Quietly*) He cleans the boots, Eugene. You will clean them tomorrow for saying that about him.

MARCHBANKS. Oh, don't talk about boots! Your feet should be beautiful on the mountains.

CANDIDA. My feet would not be beautiful on the Hackney Road without boots.

PROSERPINE. (*Enters* L, *with telegram, gives it to* MORELL *who reads it*) A telegram. It's reply paid. The boy's waiting. (*To* CANDIDA) Maria is ready for you now in the kitchen, Mrs. Morell. The onions have come.

MARCHBANKS. (*Convulsively*) Onions!

CANDIDA. Yes, onions: nasty little red onions. And you shall help me slice them. To the kitchen.

MARCHBANKS. With all my heart! (*Runs off* R)

MORELL. (*Gives telegram to* PROSERPINE) Send an answer. Tell them, "No." I will not attend the meeting tonight. (PROSERPINE *nods and exits* L)

CANDIDA. Come here, dear. Let me look at you. My boy is not looking well. Has he been overworking? Must you go out every night lecturing and talking? Of course what you say is all very true, but it does no good. The truth is, James dear, they come because you preach so splendidly. Why, it's as good as going to a play for them. And the women: why do you think they are so enthusiastic?

MORELL. (*Shocked*) Candida!

CANDIDA. Oh, I know. You think it's your sermons. They are all in love with you. And you are in love with preaching because you do it so beautifully.

MORELL. Candida: what dreadful cynicism! Or—can it be—are you jealous?

CANDIDA. Yes, I feel a little jealous sometimes. Not jealous of any of them. Jealous for somebody else, who is not loved as he ought to be.

MORELL. Me?

CANDIDA. YOU! Why, you're spoiled with love. No: I mean Eugene.

MORELL. Eugene!

CANDIDA. It seems unfair that all the love should go to you. Someone should give some to him.

MORELL. You know that I have perfect confidence in you, Candida, of your goodness, of your purity.

CANDIDA. Oh, you are a clergyman, James, a thorough clergyman!

MORELL. So Eugene says.

CANDIDA. Eugene is always right. He's a wonderful boy. I have grown fonder and fonder of him. Do you know, James, that though he has not the least suspicion of it himself, he is ready to fall madly in love with me?

MORELL. Oh, he has no suspicion of it himself, has he?

CANDIDA. Not a bit. Some day he will know, and he will know that I must have known. I wonder what he will think of me then.

MORELL. No evil, I hope.

CANDIDA. That will depend on what happens to him. If he learns love from a good woman, then it will be all right: he will forgive me. But suppose he learns it from a bad woman, as so many men do, will he forgive me for not teaching him myself? For abandoning him for the sake of my goodness and purity, as you call it? Ah, James, how little you understand me. I would give them both to poor Eugene if there were nothing else to restrain me. But there is: put your trust in my love for you, James; for if that went, I should care very little for your sermons.

MORELL. His words!

CANDIDA. Whose words?

MORELL. Eugene's.

CANDIDA. (*Delighted*) He is always right. He understands me; and you, darling, you understand nothing. (*Laughs and kisses him*)

MORELL. (*He recoils as if stabbed*) How can you bear to do that when— Oh, Candida, I had rather you had plunged a grappling iron into my heart than given me that kiss.

CANDIDA. (*Amazed*) My dear, what's the matter?

MORELL. Don't touch me.

CANDIDA. James!!

MARCHBANKS. (*Enters* R) In anything the matter?

MORELL. (*With great constraint*) Nothing but this: that either you were right, or Candida is mad.

CANDIDA. (*Relieved and laughing*) Oh, you're only shocked. Is that all? (*Gaily*) This comes of James teaching me to think for myself, and never to hold back out of fear of what other people may think of me. It works beautifully as long as I think the same things as he does. But now! because I have just thought something different look at him! Just look!

MARCHBANKS. No, you are being cruel, and I hate cruelty. It is a horrible thing to see one person make another suffer.

CANDIDA. Poor boy. Have I been cruel? Did I make it slice nasty little red onions?

MARCHBANKS. Oh, stop, stop: I don't mean myself. You have tortured him frightfully. I can feel his pain.

CANDIDA. *I?* torture James? What nonsense!

LEXY. (*Enters* L, *anxious and important*) I've just come from the Guild of St. Matthew. They are in the greatest consternation about your telegram. They've taken the large hall in Mare Street and spent a lot of money on posters, and your telegram said you couldn't come.

CANDIDA. Couldn't come! But why, James?

MORELL. (*Almost fiercely*) Because I don't choose. May I not have one night at home with my wife, and my friends?

CANDIDA. (*They are all amazed at this outburst*) Oh, do go, James. If you don't, you'll have an attack of bad conscience tomorrow. We'll all go! We'll all sit on the platform and be great people.

MARCHBANKS. (*Terrified*) No! Everyone will stare at us.

CANDIDA. They'll be too busy looking at James to notice you.

MORELL. (*Looks at* CANDIDA *and then at* MARCHBANKS; *goes to door and calls in a commanding tone*) Miss Garnett.

PROSERPINE. (*Off*) Yes, Mr. Morell. Coming. (*Enters*)

MORELL. Telegraph to the Guild of St. Matthew that I am coming. I shall want you to take some notes at the meeting. And you are coming, Lexy, I suppose?

LEXY. Certainly.

CANDIDA. We're all coming, James.

MORELL. No. You are not coming; and Eugene is not coming. You will stay here and entertain him—to celebrate your return home.

CANDIDA. But, James—

MORELL. (*Authoritatively*) I insist. You do not want to come; and he does not want to come. Oh, don't concern yourselves: there will be plenty who will want to hear me. And— I should be afraid to let myself go before Eugene. He is so critical of preaching and sermons. He knows I am afraid of him. He told me so. Well, I shall show him how much afraid I am by leaving him here in your custody, Candida.

MARCHBANKS. That is brave. That is beautiful.

CANDIDA. But—but— Is anything the matter, James? I can't understand—

MORELL. (*Taking her tenderly in his arms and kissing her on the forehead*) Ah, I thought it was *I* who couldn't understand, dear.

(*The lights dim down and out, marking a passing of several hours. When the lights dim up,* CANDIDA *and* MARCHBANKS *are sitting by the fire. He is in a small chair, reading aloud. A pile of manuscripts are on the carpet beside him.* CANDIDA *is in the easy chair. The poker, a light brass one, is upright in her hand. Leaning back and looking intently at the point of it,*

*she is in a waking dream, miles from her surround-
ings and completely oblivious of* EUGENE)

MARCHBANKS. (*Breaking off in his reading*) Every poet
that ever lived has put that thought into a sonnet. (*Looks
at her*) Haven't you been listening? (*No response*) Mrs.
Morell!

CANDIDA. Eh?

MARCHBANKS. Haven't you been listening?

CANDIDA. (*With a guilty excess of politeness*) Oh, yes.
I'm longing to hear what happens to the angel.

MARCHBANKS. I finished the poem about the angel
quarter of an hour ago.

CANDIDA. I'm so sorry, Eugene. I think the poker must
have hypnotized me.

MARCHBANKS. It made me horribly uneasy.

CANDIDA. (*She puts it down*) Why didn't you tell me?
(*He picks up another manuscript*) No, no more poems,
please. You've been reading to me ever since James went
out. I want to talk. I want to be amused. Don't you want
to?

MARCHBANKS. (*Half in terror, half enraptured*) Yes.

CANDIDA. Then come along. (*She moves her chair back
to make room*)

MARCHBANKS. (*He timidly stretches himself on the
hearth-rug, face upwards, and throws back his head
across her knees, looking up at her*) Oh, I've been so
miserable all the evening, because I was doing right. Now
I'm doing wrong; and I'm happy. There is only one word
I want to speak.

CANDIDA. What one is that?

MARCHBANKS. (*Softly*) Candida, Candida, Candida,
Candida, Candida.

CANDIDA. And what have you to say to Candida?

MARCHBANKS. Nothing but to repeat your name a
thousand times. Every time it is a prayer to you. I feel
I have come into Heaven, where want is unknown.

MORELL. (*He enters* L, *halts on the threshold, and
takes in the scene at a glance*) I hope I didn't disturb
you.

CANDIDA. (*Starts up, but without the smallest embar-*

rassment, laughing at herself. EUGENE, *capsized by her sudden movement, recovers himself without rising, and sits on the rug hugging his ankles, also quite unembarrassed*) Oh, James, how you startled me! I was so taken up with Eugene that I didn't hear your latchkey. How did the meeting go off? Did you speak well?

MORELL. I have never spoken better in my life.

CANDIDA. Good! And where are the others?

MORELL. I believe they are having supper somewhere.

CANDIDA. Oh, in that case, Maria may go to bed. I'll tell her.

(Exits R*)*

MORELL. (*Looking sternly down at* MARCHBANKS) Well?

MARCHBANKS. (*Impishly humorous*) Well?

MORELL. Have you anything to tell me?

MARCHBANKS. Only that I have been making a fool of myself here in private whilst you have been making a fool of yourself in public.

MORELL. Hardly in the same way, I think.

MARCHBANKS. (*Eagerly scrambling up*) The very, very, very same way. I have been playing the Good Man. Just like you. When you began your heroics about leaving me here with Candida—

MORELL. Candida!

MARCHBANKS. Oh, yes: I've got that far. But don't be afraid. I swore not to say a word in your absence that I would not have said a month ago in your presence.

MORELL. Did you keep your oath?

MARCHBANKS. It kept itself until a few minutes ago. Up to that moment I went on desperately reading to her —my poems—anybody's poems—to start off a conversation. I was standing outside the gate of Heaven, and refusing to go in. Oh, you can't think how heroic it was, and how uncomfortable! Then—

MORELL. Then?

MARCHBANKS. Then she couldn't bear being read to any longer.

MORELL. And you approached the gate of Heaven at last?

MARCHBANKS. Yes.

MORELL. Well? (*Fiercely*) Speak, man: have you no feeling for me?

MARCHBANKS. (*Softly and musically*) Then she became an angel; and there was a flaming sword that turned every way, so that I couldn't go in; for I saw that the gate was really the gate of Hell.

MORELL. (*Triumphantly*) She repulsed you!

MARCHBANKS. No, she offered me her wings. the wreath of stars on her head, the lilies in her hand, the crescent moon beneath her feet—

MORELL. (*Seizing him*) Out with the truth, man: my wife is my wife: I want no more of your poetic fripperies.

MARCHBANKS. (*Without fear or resistance*) Catch me by the shirt collar, Morell: she will arrange it for me as she did before. I shall feel her hands touch me.

MORELL. You young imp!

MARCHBANKS. I am not afraid now. I disliked you before. But I saw today—when she tortured you—that you love her. Since then I have been your friend. You may strangle me if you like.

MORELL. (*Releasing him*) Eugene, if you have a spark of human feeling left in you—will you tell me what has happened during my absence?

MARCHBANKS. What happened! Why, the flaming sword— (MORELL *stamps with impatience*) —Well, in plain prose, I loved her so exquisitely that I wanted nothing more than the happiness of being in such love. And before I had time to come down from the highest summits, you came in.

MORELL. So it is still unsettled. Still the misery of doubt.

MARCHBANKS. Misery! I am the happiest of men. I desire nothing now but her happiness. Oh, Morell, let us both give her up. Why should she have to choose between a wretched little nervous disease like me, and a pig-headed parson like you? Let us go on a pilgrimage, you to the east and I to the west, in search of a worthy lover for her: some beautiful archangel with purple wings—

MORELL. Some fiddlestick! Oh, if she is mad enough to

leave me for you, who will protect her? Who will help her?

MARCHBANKS. She does not ask those silly questions. It is she who wants somebody to protect, to help. Some grown up man who has become as a little child again. Don't you see, I am the man, Morell: I am the man. Send for her and let her choose between— (*He stops as if petrified when he sees* CANDIDA *enter*)

CANDIDA. (*Enters* R) What on earth are you at, Eugene?

MARCHBANKS. James and I are having a preaching match; and he is getting the worst of it.

CANDIDA. (*Sees* MORELL *is distressed, she hurries to him, greatly vexed*) You have been annoying him. I won't have it. Do you hear, Eugene, I won't have it.

MARCHBANKS. Oh, you are not angry with me, are you?

CANDIDA. Yes, I am: very angry.

MORELL. Gently, Candida, gently. I am able to take care of myself.

CANDIDA. Yes, dear, of course you are. But you mustn't be annoyed and made miserable. (*To* EUGENE) Now are you sorry for what you did?

MARCHBANKS. (*Earnestly*) Yes. Heartbroken.

CANDIDA. Then off to bed like a good boy.

MARCHBANKS. (*To* MORELL) Oh, I can't go now, Morell. I must be here when she— Tell her.

CANDIDA. Tell her what?

MORELL. (*Slowly*) I— I meant to prepare your mind carefully for this.

CANDIDA. Yes, dear, I am sure you did.

MORELL. Well—er—

CANDIDA. Well?

MORELL. Eugene declares that you are in love with him.

MARCHBANKS. No, no, no, no, never. I did not, Mrs. Morell: it's not true. I said I loved you. I said I understood you, and that he couldn't.

MORELL. And he said that you despised me in your heart.

CANDIDA. Did you say that?

MARCHBANKS. (*Terrified*) No, no, no! I— I— (*Desperately*) It was David's wife.

MORELL. He has claimed that you belong to him and not to me; and, rightly or wrongly, I have come to fear that it may be true. We have agreed—he and I—that you shall choose between us now. I await your decision.

CANDIDA. Oh! I am to choose am I? I suppose it is quite settled that I must belong to one or the other.

MORELL. (*Firmly*) Quite.

MARCHBANKS. (*Anxiously*) Morell, you don't understand. She means that she belongs to herself.

CANDIDA. I mean that, and a good deal more, Master Eugene, as you will both find out presently. And pray, my lords and masters, what have you to offer for my choice? I am up for auction, it seems. What do you bid, James?

MORELL. (*With proud humility*) I have nothing to offer you but my strength for your defence, my honesty for your surety, my ability and industry for your livelihood, and my authority and position for your dignity. That is all it becomes a man to offer to a woman.

CANDIDA. And you, Eugene? What do you offer?

MARCHBANKS. My weakness. My desolation. My heart's need.

CANDIDA. That's a good bid, Eugene. Now I know how to make my choice. (*She pauses and looks curiously from one to the other*)

MORELL. (*Appeals from the depths of his anguish*) Candida!

MARCHBANKS. Coward!

CANDIDA. I give myself to the weaker of the two. (EUGENE *divines her meaning at once: his face whitens like steel in a furnace*)

MORELL. (*Bowing his head with the calm of collapse*) I accept your sentence, Candida.

CANDIDA. Do you understand, Eugene?

MARCHBANKS. Yes. I have lost. He cannot bear the burden.

MORELL. (*Incredulously*) Do you mean me, Candida?

CANDIDA. (*Smiles*) Let us talk like three friends. You have told me, Eugene, how nobody has cared for you since your old nurse died; how miserable you were at Eton, always lonely and misunderstood.

MARCHBANKS. I had my books. I had Nature. And at last I met you.

CANDIDA. Now I want you to look at this other boy

here! Spoiled from his cradle. Ask James' mother and his sisters what it cost to save James the trouble of doing anything but be strong and clever and happy. Ask me what is costs to be James' mother and sisters and wife and mother to his children all in one. I build a castle of comfort and love for him. And when he thought I might go away with you, his only anxiety was—what should become of me! And to tempt me to stay he offered me his strength for my defence! his industry for my livelihood! his dignity for my position! his—ah, I am mixing up your beautiful cadences and spoiling them, am I not, darling?

MORELL. (*Embraces her*) It's all true, every word. You are my wife, my mother, my sisters, you are the sum of all loving care to me.

CANDIDA. (*Smiles, to* EUGENE) Am I your mother and sisters to you, Eugene?

MARCHBANKS. (*In disgust*) Ah, never. Out, then, into the night with me!

CANDIDA. You are not going like that, Eugene?

MARCHBANKS. (*With the ring of a man's voice*) I know the hour when it strikes. I am impatient to do what must be done.

MORELL. Candida, don't let him do anything rash.

CANDIDA. Oh, there is no fear. He has learnt to live without happiness.

MARCHBANKS. I no longer desire happiness. Life is nobler than that. Parson James, I give you my happiness with both hands. I love you because you have filled the heart of the woman I loved. Goodbye.

CANDIDA. One last word. How old are you, Eugene?

MARCHBANKS. As old as the world now. This morning I was eighteen.

CANDIDA. Eighteen! Will you, for my sake, make a little poem out of the two sentences I am going to say to you? And will you promise to repeat it to yourself whenever you think of me?

MARCHBANKS. Say the sentences.

CANDIDA. When I am thirty, she will be forty-five. When I am sixty, she will be seventy-five.

MARCHBANKS. In a hundred years, we shall be the

same age. But I have a better secret than that in my heart. Let me go now. The night outside grows impatient.

CANDIDA. Goodbye. (*She takes his face in her hands; and as he divines her intention and falls on his knees, she kisses his forehead. Then he flies out into the night. She turns to* MORELL, *holding out her arms to him*) Ah, James! (*They embrace. But they do not know the secret in the poet's heart*)

—The End—

OTHER TITLES AVAILABLE FROM BAKER'S PLAYS

FASHION

Anna Cora Mowatt's classic, Adapted and Abridged as a One-Act by Aurand Harris

5m, 4f / interior

One of the most popular plays of early American theatre now adapted for one-act play use. This classic contrasts the foibles of New York society and its garish imitation of foreign manners with the true Americanism of sterling rural types like Adam Trueman. The goodness and unabashed patriotism of this old farmer from Catteraugus prevail in the end against the pretension of Mrs. Tiffany - a lady who believes herself fashionable - and the schemes of a bogus Count who is finally exposed as a fortune-hunter. Melodrama, farce and sentiment combine to make a one-act of wit and charm.

OTHER TITLES AVAILABLE FROM BAKER'S PLAYS

LADIES OF THE MOP

Aurand Harris

Play in Rhyme and Rhythm

4f

Annie is a faded, fluttery woman who has not lost her dream of the stage; Mattie, an unimaginative soul with a toneless voice; Hallie, loud, robust, energetic; and Bessie, tall and dignified – sole admirer of her own voice. Annie proposes they entertain themselves while they eat their midnight snack and rest from their scrubbing of the bare stage. So Bessie sings, Hallie dances, Mattie plays a piano number and Annie gives a melodramatic reading. When, after a disagreement, all four perform simultaneously ...well, it has to be seen to be appreciated.

OTHER TITLES AVAILABLE FROM BAKER'S PLAYS

ONCE UPON A CLOTHESLINE

Aurand Harris

fantasy in four scenes / 13 characters / flexible casting / unit set

Pinno and Pinnette, two clothespins, are getting acquainted while they hold a quilt on the line, when the ugly Black Spider threatens Pinnette! Pinno rises to her defense, but in his eagerness falls to the ground. He is discovered by Mrs. and Junior Ant, and revived by Dr. Beetle with the help of some odd instruments – a saw, an axe, a bicycle pump, and a dinner bell! But no sooner is Pinno revived than Pinnette tumbles into the Spider's web! It takes all the efforts of Pinno and his hilarious posse to rescue her. Viola Spolin, author of *Improvisation for the Theatre*, says of this award-winning children's classic, "I found the play completely delightful to direct, and the young actors enjoyed every minute of it." Aurand Harris was one of the country's most popular writers of children's plays, and was the recipient of many awards including The Chorpenning Playwriting Award and an NEA Fellowship for Creative Writing.

0 1341 1464088 8

Breinigsville, PA USA
19 January 2011
253675BV00004B/4/P

9 780874 409833